AWAY AND PLAY ROUND YER OWN DURES

J B MCMULLAN

CONTENTS

ACKNOWLEDGMENTS

With thanks to Ronan and Theresa

ALL PROCEEDS IN AID OF CANCER
RESEARCH

PART I

AROUND THE TOWN

"Away and play round yer own dures yis 'ave my head near astray!"

Maggie Mason was in full battle-cry and on the war-path. Turbo, Finn and I were quickly retrieving our ball and making good our escape.

Maggie wasn't small and she wasn't tall, she wasn't fat or thin, she could perhaps be described as a fair to middling woman. She was definitely old, but as we viewed anyone over forty as old, we couldn't say how old. Her hair was frayed and grayed at the edges and tied back in a tight bun which was positioned on her head like a coxcomb. She had small darting eyes like a bird, which seemed to see everything and could read what we were whispering or saying under our breath. A sharp beak of a nose completed a somewhat avian appearance. Her thin, pursed lips were like a cat's arse from which she continued to hurl verbal abuse in our direction.

Maggie, though, had one redeeming feature she had big kerbs or, at least, the street outside her front door had. These were a pre-requisite for a good game of kerby which involved throwing a ball against the kerb-stones and catching it on the rebound. To be fair to Maggie the sound of it reverberating through the foundations probably would have put your head astray but at the time we couldn't see what she had to complain about.

Maggie lived in a small two bedroom cottage-type house in Burn Brae. Many years after this incident, which was a recurring rather than an isolated incident, the house was pulled down, when it was found that the houses there, were subsiding. If Maggie had been alive she would, no doubt, have attributed a whole row of houses subsiding to us boys playing kerby.

Maggie adhered to the principle that children should be seen but not heard and certainly not liked. It is often said that the three most important features of a house are location, location, location. Maggie could not have lived in a worse location. Her back garden was separated from the football-field by a patchy privet hedge, the side of her house abutted another small playing field in front of the police station and the front of her house had those big kerbs. She was bombarded on all sides by screaming, playing kids and with footballs entering her garden from all angles.

It has to be said that she fought back valiantly. She had two main tactics. The ball would either be taken hostage and children asking for their ball back would be given a vicious tongue-lashing, or she would simply take a hot poker from the fire, burst it, and throw it back in the direction from which it came. This must have given her some degree of satisfaction as the kids left as deflated as their ball. And this is why we were very quickly retrieving our ball before making-off. Needless to say, we did not go quietly.

"Oul' Maggie chewed tobaccy!" shouted Turbo.

This rhyming insult lacked a good punch-line finish but a further rhyme with "tobaccy" eluded us. Whenever we fired this insult at Maggie, which again was not an isolated occurrence, it seemed to just hang there without really hitting its target.

And we couldn't follow her advice to 'play round our own dures' as we were always met with:

"Away and play yerselves and get away out of my sight!" and that was from our own mothers.

Trying to pursue a free-wheeling, carefree childhood during the summer holidays was not without its difficulties.

"Let's go down to Teenie's," suggested Finn, "my aunt gave me two bob last night."

"Now yer talking" said Turbo, as he hid the ball in a hedge, to pick up later, and we headed down town.

At the corner of Anne Street and Church Street there was a street pump just beside the Brewery Yard. Some of the older houses in Church Street still had no mains water supply and relied on the pump for clean, fresh water. This particular morning a black Labrador stood barking beside the pump. It was Richard Doran's dog called Blackie. Invariably, all black dogs about the town were either called Blackie or Darkie, originality in dog-naming was still somewhat lacking. At times you heard people say 'Oh, that's Blackie's pup Blackie!'

Dickie Doran, as he was known, was a well-respected man about town. As well as the deficiency in dog-naming, we thought it was rather irresponsible of parents to christen a child Richard, for them to be known as a Dick for the rest of their lives. William wasn't much better. Dickie's progress up the street was slow as he stopped and spoke to everyone he met. Blackie knew this and despite his unoriginal name he was an original thinker. He had worked out that if he stood barking at the pump that someone would turn it on sooner than waiting for Dickie. We duly obliged but perhaps too enthusiastically. When Dickie eventually came alongside the dog shook itself soaking both us and him.

"Would you look at the state of that dog!" roared Dickie.

"He wanted a drink," said Finn.

"Well he didn't want a bath, you're three eejits you three!"

We had been called worse but still it required a response, and we chanted after Dickie:-

"Clever Dick, clever Dick make me sick,
Clever Dick, clever Dick give yer ass a lick!"

He pretended not to hear and continued on up the street, he may have smiled or he may not have but, at any rate, it amused us greatly. It was only half-past ten in the morning and we had already insulted two people, still, the day was young.

We continued our way up Church Street until we came to the small gate-lodge at the entrance to the demesne.

"Let's take a short-cut through here," said Turbo. Such short-cuts were never actually short-cuts they were just an alternative route which usually involved some form of trespass and often ended with us being caught and reprimanded. On this occasion we managed to nip through the demesne and climb a wall into the Ropewalk without incident. The Ropewalk in those years was full of old junk and old cars, an adventure play-ground for us boys, and we spent many a happy hour there. It passed alongside the Castle Gardens.

"Wow, look at the size of the apples there this year!" said Turbo excitedly.

"After getting caught and getting our asses kicked last year, there's no chance, Turbo," said Finn, putting an end to any plans that Turbo may have had of us raiding the orchard.

I readily agreed and we were content to be called 'yellow-bellies' rather than repeat the experience. We made our way slowly up the Shambles and arrived at Teenie's.

The outside of Teenie's shop was adorned with all the accoutrements necessary for a good beach holiday. Plastic buckets and spades, beach-balls, frisbees, inflatable-rings, plastic tennis-rackets and fishing-nets that usually parted company with the bamboo rod after about ten minutes. Inside it was a veritable Aladdin's Cave of toys, sweets, Walls' ice-cream and the best selection of lolly-pops in town. The Jolly Jelly, with the sliver of strawberry jelly in the centre, was our favourite. But if we could scrape enough money together our first choice was always three glasses of lemonade or even two and we would share.

For a time, we had been barred from Teenie's after Turbo had spat his lemonade into the Superser heater. However, after 'crossing our hearts and hoping to die' if we ever did anything similar again Teenie relented and we were allowed back. Unlike Maggie, Teenie liked children, and she wasn't hard to win round. I always thought that selling glasses of lemonade to children was her way of getting them to hang around for a while to enjoy a bit of chat. In the middle of the week there was not much passing trade and it must have been lonely enough at times just sitting in the shop.

"Well, did ye get yer breakfast, boys?" was Teenie's opening remark.

"Aye."

"What did you have?" It is often said that nosey people would ask you what you had for your breakfast but this was only Teenie's way of starting a conversation and not a very good one as we all had the same answer.

"Porridge!" We did, however, have a choice as regards the porridge, we could either like it or lump it. We liked it, especially when we managed to get the cream of the milk. In those days, all milk was delivered in bottles to the door-step, it was full milk and the first few inches was pure cream. Whoever was fortunate enough to be first opening the bottle was the cat who got the cream. With a heaped spoonful of sugar it made great porridge.

We all seemed to get the same dinners as well. The week revolved round mince, carrot and onion with spuds, stew, home-made soup with spuds, champ, and fish, peas and spuds on Fridays. Catholics were barred from eating meat on Fridays as it was a fast day. It always seemed to be a strange penance to us, as we didn't get much meat anyway, and a nice bit of brown fish (smoked haddock to the better educated) or herring was certainly better than mince.

There was some debate whether black pudding broke the Friday fast. There were two schools of thought, one that it was made of pig's blood, oatmeal and vegetable matter and didn't contain any meat. The second was that it did contain some form of minced off-cuts of meat. Local butchers couldn't be relied on to adjudicate fairly on the matter as no self-respecting butcher would admit to having no meat in their black puddings. And so, the matter was left to an individual's conscience.

It should also be noted that it was spuds with everything. By the late 1960s pasta and rice had still not reached Portaferry, we would not have known how to cook it or what to do with it, and we were not alone. A few years earlier the BBC had run an April Fool's hoax showing spaghetti growing on trees and they were inundated with calls asking where they could purchase such trees. Anyway, with the opening conversation about porridge quickly over we placed our order.

"Three glasses of brown lemonade, Teenie please." said Finn producing his two bob-bit. We had moved on to the hard stuff, brown lemonade, although secretly I still preferred the sweeter raspberryade. The fizz from the lemonade was powerful, it went straight up your nose, made your eyes water and often brought on a fit of hiccups.

"Teenie, how do you think they make brown lemonade?" said Finn. "Do you think they use tea-leaves to turn white lemonade brown?"

"Sure, if they did that Finn," said Teenie, "it would make the lemonade taste like tea. Lemonade straight from the fridge would be like drinking iced-tea and who would want that?"

None of us had a fridge, but we nodded solemnly in agreement, Teenie was right, iced-tea was not something that would ever catch on.

"Well, were you speaking to anyone up the street?" continued Teenie.

Teenie and Dickie were good friends so we didn't mention our slight altercation, other than agreeing that his Blackie was the smartest Blackie in town.

"Oul' Maggie was on the war-path again," said Turbo, taking another sip of his lemonade, "She was trying to burst our ball!"

"Now, I hope yis haven't been keeping her going. She hasn't her sorrows to seek. She's a widow-woman you know, mind you, she's worth a bob or two."

I noticed that every time someone mentioned that Maggie was a widow-woman it was immediately followed with 'mind you she's worth a bob or two.' Teenie went on to tell us a bit more about Maggie:

"Maggie's not from Portaferry, you know. She came over here from England with her parents when she was a child. And although she must be here now over fifty years some still consider her a 'blow-in'. It can't be easy not having any family of yer own around ye."

"She was a fine looking girl in her day and she still keeps herself very neat and tidy, gets the hair and all done every fortnight."

It was hard for us to imagine Maggie as 'a fine looking girl' or to imagine what getting her 'hair done' involved. Was it possible to get it re-bunned? We had no idea. We did see her one summer afternoon with her hair down. She was in her back garden letting it dry in the sunshine. It was nearly down to her waist, and it was a lot greyer, which made her look even more witch-like. We weren't actually sure that it was her, as she had her back to us, but we confirmed her identity by shouting 'oul' Maggie' through the hedge, which made her turn round and we were off before she could identify us.

"John Pat had a quare notion of her, at one time," continued Teenie.

John Pat was a reference to John Pat Murphy who lived at Bankmore and was a good friend of ours. We called him the man with three names as his male friends called him Pat, women-folk called him John Pat and our generation called him JP. He used to say that he didn't mind what he was called as long as it wasn't early in the morning.

"Then Tommy Mason took a fancy to her. Young Tommy, as the eldest son, had inherited the family farm. It had a large dairy herd, a wheen of acres in wheat or barley and a lock of potatoes on the go as well."

" John Pat was a good-looking lad but Tommy had the money. When it comes to money or looks boys, it's money every time."

"You'll need to earn plenty of money, then Turbo," said Finn.

"You'll need both!" retorted Turbo.

"Now boys," said Teenie in a slightly raised tone, that restored order, as no one wanted to be blamed for getting us barred again.

"Anyway, in the end Maggie picked Tommy and they were married in the Church of Ireland in the town. They were married less than a year when Tommy was killed in a tragic farm accident. Maggie couldn't run the farm by herself so she sold it to the two brothers and moved into her wee house in Burn Brae. And as I said, she's now worth a bob or two."

"So, you see you shouldn't be keeping her going, God knows she hasn't had her sorrows to seek," concluded Teenie. We thanked Teenie for the lemonade and came away thinking that perhaps, in future, we should be kinder to Maggie.

Outside the shop we launched into a burping contest, the fizzy lemonade always caused a gaseous reaction. We didn't see wee Mrs. Emerson hurrying along with her shopping basket but she soon cut a swathe through us with her walking stick.

"Bloody eejits!" she muttered under her breath, and a torrent of burps chased after her up the street.

. . .

"Let's go out Bankmore and see JP," suggested Finn and so we headed down the Virgin's Lane.

"Hey Finn, why do they call this street the Virgin's Lane?" I asked, as he tended to know about such things.

"I dunno," came his reply.

We didn't actually know what a virgin was. I had a

vague idea that it might be an unmarried mother. But even if we had known it would still not have enlightened us as to the origin of the street name. Whenever Finn was unable to answer a question of this nature Turbo was in immediately with his own theory.

"It's because the Virgin Mary appeared down this Lane. You know the way she turned up unexpectantly at Lourdes and Knock and that other place in Portugal."

"Fatima," said Finn. "My Ma went there on a pilgrimage once."

"Yea, that's it, Fatty Ma, they must have named it after yer Ma."

"Very funny, Turbo."

"Jeesus Turbo," I said, "if that was the case sure there would be a line of pilgrims from here to Kircubbin, blessing themselves and saying the rosary."

"Aye yer right, but the Protestants hushed it up. Look around ye and what do ye see?"

"A row of wee houses," I replied.

"No, on the other side – the Orange Hall and the Methodist's Meeting House!"

"The Virgin Mary always appeared on high ground so that people could see her. That's why her statue is always positioned high up in grottos. My guess is that she appeared on the rock where the Orange Hall is now built. Us Catholics couldn't very well put a statue on top of an Orange Hall , could we now?"

"And in case we tried to put it further down the street they built the Methodist's Meeting House and named the street Cuan Place. But despite that everyone still calls it the Virgin's Lane so there has to be some reason for it."

Finn, obviously not impressed with this reasoning, raised his eyes to Heaven as if the Virgin was about to appear. I wish she had, as contrary to Finn, I was very impressed with Turbo's explanation.

"Well, why do you think they call the Big Back Lane, Purgatory?" I continued.

"The Protestants again," there was no stopping Turbo now.

"Did you ever notice when coming down the Big Lane that it's always dark and dismal until it opens out and brightens up around the big Protestant Cathedral?"

"It's not a Cathedral," said Finn.

"Well whatever it is. Going from darkness into light is like going from Purgatory into Heaven and it means Heaven is to be found in the Protestant Church."

"Jeesus Turbo, those Protestants have it all sewn up!" said Finn sarcastically.

"Yea, yer right there Finn," replied Turbo triumphantly, thinking that Finn had at last seen the light.

We dandered on down Ferry Street and out on to the shore front. In the unlikely event of any of us ever getting to Heaven we thought it would be some sort of Paradise like this with the sunshine glistening on the lough and glorious sunsets sinking into it every evening.

It was always the same but always different. The ferry-boat went back and forth as it always did, someone was tinkering with a boat at the quay-side, a man standing up in a punt as it went puttering down the lough and a yacht fluttering aimlessly for lack of wind. Old men sat smoking on the sea wall and we joined them, sitting that is, not smoking. Their conversations always began with 'D'ye mind the day…' and a story that had been told and re-told down the years, now unfolded for a new generation hearing it for the first time.

Finn always maintained that the Portaferry shore-front owed everything to Strangford as the view before us was that of Strangford. Equally the view from Strangford was that of Portaferry. They had the panorama of the quaint gate-lodge guarding the Nugent Estate, the castle, the big 'Protestant Cathedral' peeping over the houses, the iconic windmill, the Saltpans and the old white-washed fishermen's cottages creeping along the shore towards Cook Street. As views go it wasn't bad.

It was not a reflection in a mirror by any means but we certainly complemented and enhanced each other's location. Any architectural horrors on either side of the Lough would reflect badly on its neighbour. The chances of that happening were virtually nil, as it seemed to us, that nothing much had changed in the past one hundred years.

We were heading for the white-washed cottages at the far end of the shore where my grandmother lived. When we walked in the smell of home-made bread filled the small house. Most people find this aroma irresistible and three ravenous boys who had last eaten a bowl of porridge some hours before were no exception; we would have killed each other to get at it.

"Would yis take a bit of soda bread, it's just out of the oven?"

"Jeesus, would we what?" I thought to myself but politely replied,

"Yea, that would be nice."

"Well, would yis take the bucket there and get me some water from the pump and it'll be ready when ye come back."

We went along the street and filled up the bucket from the pump and took it in turns to carry it back to the house. The bread with melted butter was sitting on a big plate when we returned and we tucked in. Warm fruit soda bread with melted butter, if they didn't serve that in Heaven, we would think twice about going.

"Where are yis off to now?" asked my grandmother as we got up to leave.

"We're going out to JP's," I replied.

"I'm sure he'll be glad to see yis."

I glanced quickly at my grandmother's expression to see if she was joking but I couldn't tell.

Notwithstanding that we had relatives at the Shore, we always seemed to get on well with the folk there. They were more likely to laugh than scold and could correct with a soft word rather than a harsh one.

"Jeesus, yer granny makes great bread," said Turbo.

"She makes great everything," I replied, "Apple tarts, rhubarb tarts, cakes, buns and apple dumplings at Halloween with sixpences in them."

"To be paid to eat apple dumplings," said Turbo, "now, that's the boy for me!"

Suitably refreshed we saddled up the horses and made our way past the Scotsman and on towards Bankmore. From the other side of the street we watched a woman on her hands and knees scrubbing the pavement outside her front door. She had been doing this for so many years that there was a half-moon portion of pavement, outside her house, that was a different colour and certainly cleaner than the rest of the pavement. We couldn't work out why people thought it necessary to wash the public street but it was not an uncommon practice in those years.

At the foot of the hill that led to Bankmore proper Finn suggested that we should cut across the field to the old air-raid shelter. Unsurprisingly, Turbo suggested that we should take a short-cut so that no one would see us crossing the field. This short-cut involved making our way along the beach and then scaling an almost vertical hill-side covered in blackthorn, briars and nettles. Half way up, and the worse for wear, we stopped for a rest and a view out over the Lough.

"Jeesus boys, if the Germans had invaded," said Turbo, "we could have hidden up here and they would never have found us."

"I think I would rather have been captured," said Finn, spitting on his hands to wipe the blood away from his scratched and bleeding legs.

Eventually, we made it out into the sunlight at the top, rather battered and bruised. It was a short run to the air-raid shelter and down the ladder before stretching out on the benches there to enjoy a well-earned rest. The fizzy lemonade and water in my grandmother's started to have an effect and we retired to three corners of the shelter to water the horses. As was always the case Turbo recited the mantra:-

"No matter how ye shake yer peg
The last wee drop runs down yer leg!"

And personally speaking, I found that always to be the case. The location in the old air-raid shelter moved Turbo further to an outburst of singing, with a rousing rendition of:-

"Hitler has only got one ball,
Goering has two but they are small,
Himmler has something similar,
But poor Goebbels has no balls at all."

Finn and I joined in second time round and Turbo then segued into another of his irreverent war songs:-

"Bless them all, bless them all,
The long, the short and the tall,
For we'll not be mastered,
By no Nazi bastard…"

When things quietened down Finn, as was his wont, seized the opportunity to launch into a lecture on the Second World War. Hitler, the Nazis, the U-boats, the Atlantic convoys, the superiority of the spitfire with eight machine-guns and the Battle of Britain.

"You know, rationing started in 1940 and was still going in 1954," he continued. This was the trigger for another outburst from Turbo:

"We'll eat again,
Don't know what,
Don't know when,
But I know we'll eat again,
Some sunny day."

This made Finn laugh and, thankfully, stopped him in his tracks as he gave up his history lesson, and we reprised Hitler's anatomical deficiency with another rousing rendition, accompanied by marching up and down the air-raid shelter.

If we had managed to get into the air-raid shelter

unseen it was unlikely that we would get out of it unheard. But somehow we got back on the road undetected and made our way on and on over the hill to JP's.

JP's cottage was visible from the top of the hill. If there was smoke curling from the chimney or the smell of wood-smoke on the breeze it confirmed that he was at home. JP always had a bit of a fire on the go, winter or summer, 'keeps the crows from nesting in the chimney,' he would say. The smoke signals and the pungent smell of wood-smoke both indicated that he was in residence, and not away working on a neighbour's farm, which was sometimes the case.

The cottage nestled in the Bankmore hills with an uninterrupted view over the Lough. It had white-washed walls with the door, window-sills and drain-pipe painted a dark green. The two red brick chimneys and blue slate roof, were in as good a condition as when they first looked out on that part of the Lough. There was a rope-mat at the front door which once spelt-out 'Welcome'. We pointed out to JP that it now only retained the first two letters and the last one leaving the word 'Wee' as the greeting to visitors. JP just shrugged his shoulders and said he preferred that, as not everyone was welcome, and some folk could just go and piss-off . The foot-fall that had worn the mat to its present condition proved the opposite – everyone was welcome at JP's , even us boys.

The inside of the cottage was something of a time-warp. JP hadn't added to it or taken away from it since his mother had died maybe thirty years earlier. The focal point of the living room, was an old original Irish Dresser, displaying a blue and white dinner-set that his mother had got as a wedding present, with a matching set of cups dangling from hooks across its two shelves. JP never used any crockery from the dresser, he may not even have dusted it, since his mother had passed away.

On either side of the mantle-piece was his mother's two brown and white china dogs one having lost an eye, presumably in a fight, many years ago. There was still an old chimney-crook in the fire-place which once served all the cooking requirements for the house-hold. It had fallen into disuse when JP got his gas cooker but could still be pressed into service if he ever ran out of gas.

A small scullery looked out on to the back-yard. It had a Belfast sink with two wooden drainers either side, a couple of ancient wall cupboards, a table with a worn oil-cloth covering and four non-matching chairs. The gas cooker was on the side wall where it connected to the gas tank at that side of the house.

Outside a hawthorn hedge enclosed JP's half acre of garden. The bottom part was fenced off for 'Peggy the Pig' who always seemed to have about ten piglets about her. He also had a goat and a clatter of ducks and hens scratching about the yard. JP grew all his own vegetables, in mid-summer his garden was filled with potatoes, cabbages, onions, peas, beans and more. Beyond the hawthorn hedge he owned a couple of fields where he kept a few Irish moiled cattle. He had a small punt on the beach in front of the cottage which he used for a bit of fishing and from which he worked a few lobster-pots. All in all, JP was basically self- sufficient, he had his own milk, eggs, pork, fish, chicken and vegetables.

JP's mother was from Drumguin, County Carlow and had known Kevin Barry's mother. Kevin Barry was a young Irish republican who had been executed by the British in the War of Independence in 1920. JP had lost most of his Southern brogue but there was still a lilt and musicality to his voice which greatly enhanced his reputation as a story-teller. We also noticed that he pronounced some words differently and softer than us. In particular, he would always say 'Jaysus' whereas with our harsher Northern accent it was 'Jeesus'. I don't think the real Jesus would have minded either way but, if pushed, I think he would probably have preferred JP's version.

JP had also gained the reputation as 'a good oul' chanter.' He had a classic Irish tenor voice and his song of choice, no doubt influenced by his family connections, was the ballad, 'Kevin Barry.' Men who frequented pubs and were wont to get up and sing were known and almost defined by their choice of song. Some even derived their nicknames from the song they sang. Apparently, there was a man from Killyleagh who always sang Manfred Mann's classic 'Do Wah Diddy Diddy' and he was called Diddy

Diddy for the rest of his days.

When JP sang 'Kevin Barry', grown men were known to find something in their eye when he reached the following verse:-

"Kevin Barry, do not leave us
On the scaffold you must die!
Cried his broken-hearted mother
As she bade her son good-bye."

JP was aware of the poignancy of the song and rather than put a dampener on an evening, before the applause had ended, he would launch into something like 'I'll Tell Me Ma,' some eejit would get up to dance and general frivolity would be restored. To be able to make people cry, laugh and dance was his unique talent.

His talent was widely appreciated in the ceilidh houses that were still on the go at the time. These were open houses where everyone was welcome to all hours of the morning. Some were more welcome than others. Singers, story-tellers and musicians found that there was usually something a bit stronger in their tea and a couple of custard-creams at the side of their plate. Those not in this elite group might find milky tea with a couple of Marie biscuits. The Marie biscuit was a thin, timid type of biscuit and the worse dunking biscuit ever made. It seemed to be frightened of warm tea and immediately wilted and fell into the cup when the two were introduced.

Invariably, they would be scooped out or poured into a saucer and slurped up like a pig at the trough. Among those in the lesser group were those who took the opportunity to criticise all and sundry. They could be heard saying something like:-

"Yer man hasn't a clue what to do with that sick cow!"

And when 'yer man' walked in, it would be:-

"How's the cow coming along?"

"Ah, it's up and about like a good 'un."

"Sure, wasn't I just saying you're the boy to get it back on its feet."

The older generation had a term to describe such two-faced people, it was that, 'they're all sugar and all shite.' Such local descriptive phrases usually said it all and required no further explanation or elaboration.

Another group who were welcomed perhaps less enthusiastically at the ceilidh house was older single men, usually farmers but not exclusively. These men had been on their own too long, without the guidance of a good woman, and had lost all social graces. They tended to bring the smell of the farmyard with them, as well as clabber on their boots. They hogged the fire, spat into it and farted with impunity.

Flatulence, in itself, was not totally frowned upon as Arty Farty Mageean had made a name for himself in that sphere. He had perfected the technique of setting fire to his own farts and was much sought after as ceilidh house entertainment. Arty maintained that he needed three or four bottles of stout to 'crank up the engine.' He would sit quietly consuming his required in-take of alcohol, until he gave the signal and the sofa would be cleared, and the lamps turned down. He then lay back, drew his knees up to his chest and lit his lighter with his right hand in the general region of his posterior. JP said that on a good night you could have lit your pipe from the blue methane flame. After the cheering and applause had died away Arty would say,

"That's through two layers of cloth. Ye should see it when I'm bare-arsed!"

No one, as far as I am aware, ever took him up on his offer. Although at one time plans were afoot for him to give a performance at a concert in the Parochial Hall, not bare-arsed, I hasten to add. Unfortunately, the parish priest got wind of it, so to speak, and deemed it unsuitable entertainment for a Parochial Hall. Us boys would have paid good money to see such entertainment and I am sure we would not have been alone. In fact, we did try to recreate it ourselves but only managed to burn our bare legs and nearly cause ourselves a hernia trying to squeeze wind out. We concluded that it was too dangerous an activity for us and best left to the experts like Arty.

We found JP where we usually found him, in his vegetable garden. He was planting his soup veg of leeks, celery, parsley, carrots and parsnips. JP always said to plant summer veg in spring and winter veg in summer. His task today, was to ensure that he would have the ingredients for a good hearty soup or broth, come the long, cold days of winter.

Men of JP's age, who worked the land, wore what might be described as a country-man's uniform: stout black boots, baggy trousers from an old suit, a shirt with sleeves rolled up and a knitted sleeveless jumper with cable stitching. On colder days a jacket of a suit, not necessarily matching the trousers, and a cap completed the uniform. This changed very little when JP went into town for a few bottles of stout on a Saturday evening. It was a cleaner shirt and tie, a better suit, and the finishing touch for his man-about -town look, was a hat cocked on his head at a jaunty angle.

"Ah, it's the three wise men!" said JP when he saw us coming down the garden towards him. As we were usually called three eejits we rather liked this appellation and thought it suited us. Turbo had even suggested that we should call each other Gold, Frankenstein and Mare but as no one wanted to be called Mare, it never took off.

We sat watching JP planting his soup veg, until he eventually straightened up, took a large white handkerchief from his pocket, or what used to be a white handkerchief, and mopped the sweat from his brow and face.

"Now, would you take a drop of porter or water?" said JP.

"Porter," we all replied and trooped into the small scullery and sat down at the table. JP filled three mugs and set them down on the table.

"I think this is water JP," said Turbo.

"Ach, I'm always doing that. Ye know the way Jaysus could change water into wine, well I do the opposite, I change porter into water!"

We didn't mind as the water was so much better than the town water. It came from a well in the yard, that was fed from a natural spring, and was always freezing cold even on a warm day. If gulped down quickly, it made your head spin, or maybe that was the porter in it!

"How many boiled eggs could ye eat, Turbo?" asked JP.

" 'bout half a dozen I suppose," replied Turbo.

With that JP produced the biggest duck egg any of us had ever seen. It was in a mug rather than an egg-cup which he set on the table.

"Well, could ye ate six of them boys? It's from a young ostrich that I'm rearing." We didn't think JP had an ostrich but really we couldn't be sure.

"Jeesus JP, sure that would be a feed for a bull-calf," said Turbo, lifting the egg out of the mug to feel its weight.

"Well, yer right there, I mix them up with meal and feed them to the calves." The three of us tucked into the big egg, it tasted much stronger than a hen's egg but with some salt and butter it was palatable enough.

"Now, would ye take a drop of goat's milk to wash that down?" asked JP.

"Fecking sure we wouldn't," replied Turbo, speaking authoritatively for all of us. "I'm not sure yer milking that goat properly, the last time we tried that milk it tasted like stallions' water."

"How would you know what stallions' water tasted like?" said Finn.

"Good point Finn," laughed JP.

"Well, I smelt it that time we were caught in McNabb's yard and that goat's milk tasted just like that smell."

"Good point, Turbo," I added.

"Well, any craic with yis, today?" asked JP. I think he enjoyed us calling in as he lived in a fairly remote location and, at the very least, it gave him a break from the garden. My grandmother may have been right that he would be glad to see us. We told him that we had stopped for a drink in Teenie's earlier on and that oul' Maggie had chased us. We didn't reveal that we knew he had a 'quare notice' of her at one time.

"Och now, ye shouldn't be bothering Margaret, she's had it tough enough. She was a young widow, mind you, she's worth a bob or two."

"Did ye know Maggie when she was younger?" enquired Finn.

"Aye, I used to do a bit of work on and off for her husband Thomas. In those days we all liked to work for Tommy Mason as there was no one put the grub up like Margaret."

"At tay-breaks she used to come out to the field

with a farm boy leading a donkey and cart. She had freshly baked wheaten bread, soda bread, farm butter, cheese, buttermilk, tay, a bottle of stout for the men and lemonade for any young lads."

"When we finished in the evening we were sat down at a big table in the barn for cabbage, ham and spuds. Mind you, the ham on yer plate was near the half-side of a pig, and not that streaky bacon ye got up at Nugent's."

"Thomas used to say, jokingly to her, 'by the time ye feed all them bucks, sure I'll not have a penny left!'"

"And what happened her husband?" continued Finn.

"Ach, it was one of those tragic farm accidents that just happen. At the heels of the hunt Maggie sold the farm to Thomas' two brothers and that's why she's worth a bob or two."

"Mind you, I witnessed a farm accident up at Nugent's one time," said JP, changing the subject rather quickly from Thomas Mason.

JP in his slow , story-telling manner, proceeded to relate the tale of how wee Micky Johnston had lost his arm while working at Nugent's. Long story short, Colonel Nugent had purchased a new threshing machine, the best in the country at the time. It was painted red, blue and gold, a monster of a machine, that sent up dark puffs of smoke each time it swallowed a sheaf of barley. The sheaves went in one end and the corn shot out into bags at the other.

It could do the work of about ten men although it took about ten men to keep it supplied with sheaves. At the time of the accident JP was forking the sheaves up to wee Micky who was standing on the thresher platform, unbundling the sheaves and feeding them into the machine. It was hard, dusty, noisy work and by the end of the day everyone, including the machine, was growing tired. Then suddenly the machine stopped going with a sheaf of barley in its mouth. Wee Micky tried to free the sheaf, just as the machine started up again, and it tore his arm completely off.

"Poor wee Micky," said JP, "he was an 'armless cratur!"

I think this was probably the punch-line of the story but too subtle for boys of our age.

"And did he die?" asked Finn.

"No, he didn't and here by God didn't his arm grow back again!"

"Jeesus, JP," I never heard of a limb growing back," said Finn in amazement.

JP explained that it didn't just grow back on its own but it required several different treatments. Firstly, Micky had to go to a faith-healer, a seventh son of a seventh son, and he applied his healing powers to the missing limb, if that was indeed possible. Secondly, he had to get some soil from Father O'Doran's grave in Ballytrustan and rub it on the affected area.

"Do all priests have healing powers?" asked Finn

who was avidly engrossed in the story.

"No, but Father O'Doran was a special priest and he was responsible for so many miraculous cures he should really have been made a Saint or, at least, a Pope." We whole-hearted agreed with JP, at the very least, being made Pope shouldn't have been out of the question.

"There's a saying," continued JP, "that when a 'man of the cloth' is touching cloth he has a cure for warts, farts and broken-hearts."

Unsurprisingly, this cure was seldom accessed as it required a priest of regular habits and a house-keeper who was prepared to share such intimate information. Finally, Micky had to bless himself three times a day for three weeks, with holy-water from St. Cooey's Wells.

"Which arm did he lose?" asked Finn.

"It was the right one."

"Well how could he bless himself then, if he blessed himself with his left hand, sure that's the sign of the Devil and he would never be cured."

"I think," said JP, "that the work by the faith-healer and Father O'Doran had started sufficient growth to allow him to bless himself."

We had not quite grasped the art of story-telling, namely, to never let the facts get in the way of a good story. We always came away from JP's trying to work out what was fact and what was fiction, he wove them together so expertly, that he may not have known himself at times. He, undoubtedly, tested his stories on us, as the innocence of children pursued all the obvious questions which allowed him to adjust the tale as necessary. I thought, when this story reached the ceilidh houses, that wee Micky would probably have lost his left arm to avoid any convoluted explanation of how he blessed himself.

...

Having said our farewells to JP we were back on the road and St. Cooey's Wells were obviously our next stopping point. Needless to say, we took a short-cut at Barhall and ended up at the World War Two look-out post at Ballyquintin. This post was used during the war years to monitor shipping movements. It had a commanding view over the Lough and with golden corn-fields running down to the shore-line and the Mourne Mountains beyond, it was a most scenic location. While it was idyllic on a summer's day it was also, by its purpose and nature, very exposed. It was basically a concrete block with no windows or doors and the wind blew right through it. For those manning it, during the dark winter nights of the war years', it would have been freezing.

This historic location, once again, brought on Finn's WW2 fervour and he was now pretending to be Spitfire Paddy circling the look-out post with Turbo and I trying to shoot him down. Spitfire Paddy was an Irish fighter pilot named, Brendan

Finnucane, who flew with a shamrock painted on his spitfire. He had brought down nearly thirty enemy aircraft, before being shot-up over France, and ditching without trace in the English Channel. He was Finn's hero and there was no stopping him as he launched attack after attack on the look-out post. Eventually, Turbo intercepted him and brought him down with a sustained outburst of farting.

"Jeesus, those duck eggs would tear the arse out of ye!" said Turbo. "If Arty had got a couple of them boys in him he would have burnt the house down."

Spitfire Paddy rose from the long grass to make a final pronouncement:-

"The first spitfire to be downed by a gas attack!" and accepting his fate he fell down dead.

Finn eventually rose from the dead and we continued to make our way towards St Cooey's Wells by taking a short-cut along the shore-line and then crossing some fields. The easier route was by road but no one said it had to be easy. The access either way was difficult enough as the Wells were becoming overgrown and almost forgotten. It had been the site of an ancient church dating back to the 7th Century. All that was left now were a few foundation stones and some upright stones that marked the graves in an old graveyard. We made our way through the reed-beds that skirted the shore-line to the penitential stone which was a flat rock bearing two indentations. It was said that the indentations were made by St. Cooey kneeling on that spot while praying. We tried it for ourselves and readily agreed that it was a rock and a hard place; we certainly wouldn't have wanted to be kneeling there any longer than it took to say a Hail Mary.

There were three separate holy wells, for washing, bathing eyes and for drinking. There was a certain aura about the place, at times, you could feel the silence. We tended to speak quietly, in much the same way as one would do in an empty church, it was not a place to be shooting down any spitfires.

As we had trekked quite a few miles on a rather warm day, Finn and I took off our shoes and socks to bathe our feet in the cool water, while Turbo was drinking from the adjacent well. While sitting with our feet in the water I noticed that the flow of the water meant that Turbo was actually drinking the water that we had our feet in. I refrained from mentioning this and the peace and serenity of the place was maintained.

Fully refreshed we lay down on the grassy slopes beside the wells, watching the clouds pass over-head, and listening to the bees buzzing about the briars.

"Why do you think St. Cooey was made a Saint and Father O'Doran wasn't?" I asked.

"Maybe he had more cures," said Finn.

"Well, they both helped wee Micky."

"I don't believe that story. He could never have blessed himself without his right arm."

"I suppose anyone who kneels long enough on a rock to put two dents in it deserves to be made a

Saint," concluded Finn.

Turbo who had been half dozing, opened one eye and said,

"I wouldn't be surprised if the Protestants hadn't something to do with it."

"And why am I not surprised that you would think that," said Finn.

"Hey, I've an idea!" said Turbo, who had obviously been thinking about something else, rather than trying to resolve the mystery of the missing Saint.

"Let's get Maggie and JP back together again."

"And why would we do that," said Finn.

"Well, they were both very fond of each other when they were young and they're both now on their own."

"And what's in it for us?"

"Well, if they marry and move to Bankmore, Maggie gets JP, and we get the big kerbs."

"And, how would we get them together, Turbo?"

"I dunno, I'll have to think about it and come up with a plan."

Turbo thinking and planning sounded ominous but we saddled up the horses for the ride into town.

As we passed Ballytrustan graveyard, the final resting place of Father O'Doran, we saluted the man who should have been made a Saint or even a Pope. By contrast, we gave a different type of salute while passing our old primary school, being more than glad to have left it behind.

"Hey, let's get something in the wee shop," said Finn, "I've still a tanner left out of my two bob." The wee shop beside the chapel was the final outpost of civilization and an oasis for rambling boys.

" What about getting some Sambos?" I suggested.

Sambo was an inappropriate name, in less enlightened times, for black bubble-gum. It had a sweet aniseed flavour but was actually useless for blowing bubbles. On that basis alone it was ruled out in favour of sixpence worth of sweets out of the big sweetie-jars on the shelves behind the counter. When the door of the shop opened it triggered a bell which alerted Hannah, the shopkeeper, to our arrival.

"Well, boys it's a warm day," she said as she took up her position behind the counter. Hannah was very much like Teenie and had great patience with children. Although the shop was the furthest outpost from town it was also closest to the boys' and girls' primary schools. As a result, she was well used to children with, pennies and half-pennies, not being able to make up their minds as to what to spend their life savings on. If one was dithering she moved onto the next and came back with a smile and a suggestion.

A big favourite was the penny-mine. This was a lump of white or pink rock and, as the name suggests, some of the lumps had a penny inside. It was very hard and sweet and not at all conducive to good dental care. But the prospect of getting the lump of rock, plus your penny back, was often irresistible. The penny-mines were also kept in the big sweetie-jars and children were allowed to pick the actual lump that they wanted. The jar would be subject to close scrutiny in the hope of spotting the brown edge of a penny in the rock. Even if someone picked a lump right at the bottom of the jar, Hannah would empty the whole jar out onto the counter to ensure that they got the one they wanted. But that was primary school stuff and anyway we had a tanner.

"Could we have a drink of water?" said Finn politely. "Sure, you can," said Hannah as she went into the back of the shop that was, in fact, her kitchen and living -room.

"Jeesus, you should have asked for lemonade," whispered Turbo. Hannah returned with a big jug of water and a plastic beaker which was passed round and the jug was duly emptied.

"Well, have yis made yer minds up?"

"Could we have sixpence worth of sweets," said Finn "a mixture of them."

"Sure, you can," said Hannah as she started to fill a paper bag with one or two sweets out of each jar: butter balls, brandy balls, aniseed balls, rhubarb and custard, clove-rock and some gob-stoppers. Very pleased with our renewed supplies we thanked Hannah and made for home. Just around the corner from the wee shop we encountered some real horses at McNabb's Stud Farm. In the fields fronting onto the road were some very fine thorough-breds which we were standing admiring, when Turbo shouted.

"Jeesus, look at that horse it's having a foal!" And

sure enough, there was a foal's leg visible from beneath the horse. "Let's go and tell McNabb," said Turbo.

I wasn't sure that this was a good idea. He had previously caught us in the yard and very quickly threw us out, when all we were doing, was trying to see the horses mating. Despite my reservations we ran down the loanen leading to McNabb's yard. We found him coming out of one of the out-houses in an over-sized pair of wellingtons with a bucket of meal in his hand.

"Hey, Mister McNabb, one of yer horses is having a foal up in the field," said Turbo, breathless from running.

Without speaking he took off up the loanen with the big wellingtons walloping about his legs. I wasn't actually sure if they were big wellingtons or if he just had short legs, or perhaps both. When we caught up with him, he shouted:-

"Which horse was it?"

"That big brown and white one," said Turbo.

"Dammit sowl, how could that have a foal, it's a stallion!"

"But we saw a foal's leg!" pleaded Turbo.

"That wasn't a foal's leg it was its feckin' willy, ye eejits!"

He stormed off back down the loanen, almost like a cartoon character with the steam rising out of his head and the big wellies nearly tripping him up. Such ingratitude we thought, after all we were only trying to be helpful, Turbo roared after him:-

" Oul' McNabb from Parson's Hall
Ate the praties skins and all!"

I doubt if he even heard as he thundered on down the lane.

"Jeesus, that horse had a quare dick on it," said Finn, as we recovered our composure from McNabb's outburst, and sauntered on down the hill towards Knocknagow.

At the entrance to Knocknagow there was a wooden bench-seat where two old friends, Patsy and Jamesy, sat pursuing their favourite past-time of smoking and chatting to anyone passing by or who would sit down and join them for a while. We were more than glad to join them on the bench.

"Well, what our yis up to today?" said Patsy. We told them about the McNabb incident and they descended into uncontrollable fits of laughter. They must have got us to repeat the story three or four times.

"And what did McNabb say?

"He near went buck mad!"

"And what did you say…"

They pursued every detail and found each telling funnier than the one before. When the coughing, laughing and smoking ebbed for a moment, Jamesy asked, almost in a whisper:-

"And er, what was the horse's appendage like?"

"Do ye mean its dick?" said Turbo.

"Aye, the very man."

"Well, to tell ye the truth, at the start I thought the horse had five legs as its appendix, as you call it, was nearly touching the ground. And then I thought that it must be a foal that was coming out and we ran like hell to tell McNabb."

This sent Patsy and Jamesy into another paroxysm of laughing and coughing from which we thought they may not recover. Eventually, Finn deemed it an opportune time to offer them a sweet, in the hope that sucking a sweet would restore some calm, before one of them had a heart attack. Patsy took a brandy ball, his favourite he said, Jamesy declined as he tried to get his pipe going again. Popping the brandy ball in his mouth Patsy gave us a grave warning:

"Never mix a brandy ball with wine-gums. The combined effect of brandy and wine would land ye on yer back."

We were very glad of his advice as we would give it a go at the next earliest opportunity. We got up to leave and Jamesy gave us a shilling.

"Here, that's for the best story we've heard in a long time and, mind you, we've been sitting here a long time."

We were in no doubt that the next person who sat down would be regaled with the McNabb escapade and no doubt there would be more added to it by those two boys. I came away thinking that when us boys got old, we would be sitting on a bench somewhere, smoking pipes, laughing and saying, "D'ye mind the day we went to McNabb's…"

We parted at the head of the town for our separate houses but probably to get the same dinner of mince, carrot and onions.

"Hey Finn, don't forget yer ball," I shouted after him as he made for home.

"Ah feck!" Finn had to make another detour to Burn Brae and back and it had already been a long day.

PART II

THE MATCHMAKERS

The next day dawned as all the days seemed to dawn during the summer holidays, warm and sunny. The sun came up over Knockinelder Bay, hung about the town all day, heating up the pavements and melting tar on the road, before creeping down the sky and going for dip in the Lough in the evening to cool down. I don't recall ever sitting inside watching the rain run down the window, as we tend to do nowadays, but it may be remembered through rose-coloured sun-glasses.

The town was already on the move. Working men had left for building sites around the peninsula and farther afield. Women who had finished making the breakfast and thrown the children out to play, hoping not to see them again until tea-time, were down the street getting the bits and pieces necessary for that tea-time. When they returned home to get on with the daily chores the town was largely left to old folk, young folk and shop-keepers. There may have been the odd tourist passing through but they were a lesser-spotted, if not, an endangered species.

Children were already gathering in the football field, and making plans to go swimming later in the day, at Knockinelder or South Bay. I was there when Turbo and Finn arrived and we adjourned to the grassy banks to hear Turbo's master-plan on how to get JP and Maggie back together.

"I've worked out a cunning plan," said Turbo, "we'll offer to tidy-up Maggie's back garden." Finn and I looked at each other but said nothing until we could see where this was going.

"When we're doing her garden we'll casually mention how JP still likes her and when we go out to JP's we'll let him know how Maggie still likes him and we'll see how things develop."

"But neither of them have ever said that," I pointed out.

"No, you know that and I know that, but Maggie and JP don't know that!"

"There's a name for what we're doing, you know," said Finn.

"What's that, telling lies?" I suggested.

"No, it's matchmaking."

And so, not without some trepidation, the would-be matchmakers approached Maggie's door. "Let me do the talking," whispered Turbo. Finn and I were more than happy to comply as we were actually afraid of Maggie. Turbo had some talents, some real and some imagined, but there was no one better at chatting up old ladies. We knocked the door and stood well back.

I am not sure if Maggie actually hid behind the door, ready to pounce on small boys, but on the first rap the door was flung open and there she was as sharp and eagle-eyed as ever.

"Yis are early at it this morning. No ye can't have yer ball back!" To describe Maggie as formidable does not really do her justice, and while Finn and I were ready to run away, Turbo remained cool under pressure.

"We're not looking a ball Maggie, we were wondering if you would like us to tidy up yer back garden?" Maggie looked at us suspiciously, with her small beady eyes, almost in disbelief, and the pause allowed Turbo to continue.

"We've been doing up old age pensioners' gardens during our summer holidays and thought we would ask you?"

"Old age pensioners, indeed," said Maggie haughtily. "Well, ye wouldn't be getting any money if that's what yer after."

"No, and we wouldn't be accepting any either," said Turbo telling a bare-faced lie.

Maggie sharply scrutinized us again unsure whether to accept or decline the offer. She was not used to random acts of kindness, and it seemed to confuse her, but in the end she relented and let us in the side-gate to the back garden.

"I'll get ye some tools," she said, as she went into the back-shed and returned with a rake, a bull-hook and a pair of hedging shears, which were all old and rusting through lack of use and care.

The grass was about knee high and a petrol mower could not have tackled it and so it had to be hand-to-hand combat. We set about the task with great gusto. Turbo grabbed the grass as if it was the hair of a cowboy's head that an Indian was scalping and delivered cutting blows with the bull-hook. The old shears that I was using, after a while, started to loosen up as they remembered their purpose in life, while Finn was busy raking what we were cutting. The recent warm weather had made the grass very dry which made the cutting somewhat easier and we were making good progress. We even unearthed an old summer-seat that had been buried in a corner of the garden and had obviously long been forgotten.

After slashing and flailing at the grass for more than an hour we had about half the garden cut and we sat down on the summer-seat for a rest. Maggie, who had been closely monitoring progress from the kitchen window, arrived out with a tray on which she balanced three glasses of pineapple lemonade and a box of biscuits. She handed us a glass each and opened the tin of biscuits. JP was right about her when it came to the grubbing, albeit after we had had about three biscuits each, she wisely put the lid back on the box. The lemonade was the type that was bought from the lemonade-man who did his rounds on a Friday, and it was ice-cold, unlike us Maggie must have had a fridge. Turbo smacked his lips savouring the refreshing drink.

"Don't burp, Turbo," whispered Finn, as he made his opening move.

"I wonder how many pineapples it takes to make one bottle of lemonade, Maggie?"

"Now, how would I know that Turbot?"

"It's Turbo," corrected Finn.

"Oh, I thought yer name was something to do with fish, yer wild for the nicknames in Portaferry. People are named after fish, birds, animals, songs, there's wee this and big that!"

"Half the time I don't know if it's a real name or a nickname and the other half when I know it's a nickname I don't know the real name."

"Well, nicknames are very important, Maggie," said Finn unable to resist an explanation and gaining some confidence around Maggie.

"There are so many people in Portaferry with the same surnames and with big families there are many who end up with the same Christian name and surname. The nicknames are, therefore, important to distinguish between families and individuals."

"Traditionally, a son is very often given the same name as his father, so one is called 'big' and the other 'wee', or senior and junior."

"What happens if junior then has a son with the same name," I added, probably unhelpfully.

"Well, he would be known as 'wee junior' or even acquire a nickname of his own, which proves my point."

Maggie was obviously not used to the aimless musings and ramblings of children but I thought she was beginning to warm to it just as Turbo struck the first blow in our quest.

"JP was asking about ye, Maggie."

"And who has the nickname JP?" returned Maggie.

"John Pat Murphy of Bankmore. He's a good friend of ours and we help him in the garden sometimes."

"He said when he worked on yer farm that the grubbing you put up couldn't be bate even by Nugent's."

"When it was a ham and cabbage dinner ye got the full back-side of a pig and not just a streaky rasher."

"I think he said nearly half the side of a pig," corrected Finn.

"Well, he said there was no one like ye anyway," said Turbo, making his closing remarks.

"Did he now?" said Maggie curtly, though I noticed her twiddling with a few stray hairs that escaped the confines of her bun and I think she was pleased enough.

Turbo explained that we would be back the next day to finish the garden as we had promised wee Mrs. Emerson that we would make a start on her garden today as well. This, of course, wasn't true as there was no way that Mrs. Emerson was getting her garden done after her abusing us yesterday. It was part of the plan to continue an ongoing communication between Maggie and JP.

...

"You know, she's not a bad oul' spud," said Turbo, as we made our way up Anne Street. I wouldn't say that we were easily bought, but it was remarkable how lemonade and biscuits could mend relationships, when only the day before we had been calling Maggie all sorts of names. We turned into High Street and decided to spend the shilling that Jamesy had given us in Bobby Lennon's shop.

"Well lads?" said Bobby.

"Three Milky Ways and three penny chews," said Finn slapping the shilling down on the counter.

"Three Milky Ways at three pence each, that's nine pence and three penny chews brings it to twelve – a shilling! By God yer the boys can count."

When it came to the cost of sweets we could do the maths even if we were working in pennies and half-pennies most of the time. Except for Finn the maths at school didn't come quite as easy. I considered anything after the decimal point to be in the half-penny region and not really that important. For some reason maths teachers thought it was terribly important and that's where our opinions and capabilities differed.

"Well, tell me this," said Bobby, "how much would it cost me to buy twenty Milky Ways?"

"Five bob," said Finn, almost before Bobby had finished the question.

"Well, that's where yer wrong Finn."

"No, I'm not! Twenty Milky Ways at three pence each is sixty pence which is five bob."

"Well, put it another way," said Bobby, "if I bought them at five bob and sold them at three pence each, how much would I make?"

"Nothing," said Finn.

"Precisely, I don't buy them for five bob, I sell them for five bob!"

He wouldn't tell us what he did actually buy them for and, therefore, we remained ignorant of his profit margins. Our best guess was that he probably bought them for two pence each and made one penny a sale. With our lesson in business-studies over for the morning we headed for the shore-front.

As usual, there were a couple of old-timers sitting on the wall watching over the Lough, in case there was a tsunami, and they would have to quickly alert the townsfolk. We sat down beside them.

"I heard yis called in with McNabb yesterday," said the one sitting nearest to us. In a small town news travels faster than a tsunami.

"Aye," said Turbo, without any elaboration and we moved further along the wall to avoid any further discussion on that topic. I could see the old guys laughing to themselves, they knew, that we knew what they knew, and were amused that their reference to it needled us.

Our next move was, obviously, to check in with JP and tell him the nice things that Maggie hadn't said about him. We decided to kill two birds with the one stone and go swimming when we were out as far as Bankmore. As it was almost a four mile hike from Burn Brae to Bankmore and back we decided to use our bikes, so we returned home for bikes, towels, trunks and something to eat.

None of us had ever owned a new bike which was the case for most kids about the town. I had gained a reputation, through trial and error, as a 'fixer-upper' of old bikes and would often be called upon to fix punctures, broken chains and brakes. I had built up a stock of old wheels, tyres, tubes and other bits and pieces that could come in useful. Most of it had come from the Cloughey Road dump, which was a treasure trove, for useful parts.

In fact, this was the origin of Finn's bike. We had found an old racing frame at the dump and put it together. The back wheel was bigger than the front and we turned the racing-handlebars the other way round so that they resembled a cow's horns. We could never understand why racing-cyclists preferred to bend over the handlebars as we found it to be back-breaking. It was a unique bike but very serviceable and quick. Turbo also had a sturdy enough bike but no brakes. In those days, brakes were an optional extra and Turbo preferred to use the sole of his gutty to slow down, particularly, for the sound it made on loose gravel.

I owned a big black bike named Big Bertha. It was, apparently, a World War One bike which would have made it about fifty years old. My granda bought it from a man in a pub, I am not sure if money changed hands or just a couple of bottles of stout. All the allied forces used bicycles during the First World War. Britain had manufactured 100,000 such bikes, some were folding bikes to make them easier to carry. When the war descended into trench warfare they were still used away from the mud and the blood for reconnaissance and to carry messages quickly between trenches. It is thought that Britain's first casualty was, John Parr, who was a reconnaissance cyclist and still a teenager at the time.

Big Bertha was a heavy brute of a bike. The leather saddle, after fifty years, had no flexibility left and it was like sitting on a brick. On swimming-days I tied my towel around it to provide some padding. Invariably it worked loose and caught in the spokes, causing a tumble, but that was just something to be expected and accepted. Turbo often said, that if he had a machine-gun strapped to the handlebars, he would have taken on any German tank and I had no doubt that he would have.

Today, Big Bertha was on a victory parade along the shore-front as we cycled towards Bankmore enjoying the fresh breeze blowing up from the Lough.

When we arrived at JP's we threw the bikes down, with a clatter, and went round to the back of the house expecting to find him in the garden. He was in the scullery and the noise had alerted him to our arrival.

"Ah, it's the three wise man from the town."

"We're going swimming up the road," said Turbo, "and we just called in for a water break."

The same mugs that we had drank from the day before were produced and we sat down at the table.

"Well, what are yis up to today?"

"We were tidying-up Maggie's back garden all morning," said Finn, JP looked rather puzzled after what we had previously said about her.

"Ye were right about the grubbing JP, she gave us lemonade and a full box of biscuits," added Finn.

"Ach, she's not a bad oul' spud," continued Turbo, "she was asking about ye."

"Was she, indeed?"

"Aye, she said ye were the best worker they had on the farm and that ye were always a gentleman, I think they were her very words."

Unlike Maggie, JP's face could not conceal his emotions and he was beaming from ear to ear.

"Hey, JP have ye a tin, a pin and a couple of matches?" asked Finn.

"What do ye want those for?"

"We're going to cook up some wullicks on the beach after we have a swim."

JP produced the said items, still smiling at what

Maggie hadn't said about him.

"Be careful with them matches the ground's so dry it could all go up in flames."

There was nothing that Finn would have liked more so Turbo took the matches into safe-keeping. We thanked JP, mounted our steeds and pushed on up the road, eventually turning down a loanen leading to the beach. Normally, the loanen would have been filled with puddles and mud but it was completely dry. It was still rough and rutted from tractor tracks but Big Bertha took it in her stride and Turbo and Finn also managed to stay upright until we reached the shoreline.

The shore at Bankmore was stony and rocky so we set up camp in the field running down to the beach. The water in Strangford Lough was always freezing, JP maintained that moving water couldn't be heated and the water in Strangford Lough was always rushing in and out. He thought that we should build a dam across to Killard Point, and then we would have a warm lake to swim in during the summer and we could skate on it in the winter when it froze over. We thought this was a great idea, but that he was taking it a bit far to suggest, that it could also generate enough electricity to light up the town.

We changed into our swimming gear and made our way to the water's edge. At that point there was a small sailing boat turning to catch the wind and tide back up the Lough, and we could hear the water gurgling and talking under its planks, which made the water seem even more inviting. Unfortunately, it didn't make it any warmer, but once the tide mark got above swimming-trunk line we either warmed up or it was just so cold we couldn't feel it any longer. We were all fairly good swimmers, being pushed in at the Ferry Terminal, which was considered fun rather than dangerous meant you could either sink or swim, and we chose to swim.

After swimming and splashing around for about an hour we went shivering back to camp only to find that our clothes were missing. There was a farmer further up the field and we decided to ask him.

"Hey Mister, did you take our clothes?" asked Finn.

"And did you take the liberty to trespass in my field?" he replied.

"They're over there below the hedge, did ye want the cattle to trample all over them. Get them and get out!" he said rather sternly.

Finn gathered up the clothes and we headed back down the field. Unnoticed, he dropped a pair of underpants which Turbo quickly lifted and concealed. After a quick drying-off Turbo and I were fully dressed and Finn was still looking for his underpants.

"I bet yer man took them," said Turbo. Finn tied his towel around his waist and we marched back up the field.

"Hey Mister, did you take my underpants?"

"Ye what?"

"My underpants, they're missing, have you got

them?"

"What would I want with yer underpants?"

"I dunno, but I didn't come out this morning bare-arsed!"

"And do ye think your underpants would fit me? Now, I told yis before get on yer bikes and get out!"

"Nah, they wouldn't fit yer fat arse!" said Finn, under his breath.

"What did ye say?"

"Nothing," and we marched back down the field.

"He's a knicker-nicker," laughed Turbo.

"Why don't ye report him to the police and get the knicker-nicker nicked," I added.

Finn didn't find any of it funny, he was thinking how he was going to explain to his Ma, that he had his underpants on when he left in the morning, but none when he returned home.

"Hey Finn, look!" said Turbo pretending to retrieve the underpants from the grass. "We must have dropped them on the way down the field. Maybe ye should go back and apologise to yer man."

"Feckin' sure I'm not," said Finn struggling to get the underpants pulled up over his wet legs.

We admired the way Finn had stood up for his rights, leaving aside the fact, that he wasn't in the right. None of us had reached that point of maturity where we would apologise if we were in the wrong, and we went on castigating the poor farmer who had only, helpfully, taken our clothes out of harm's way.

With all underpants now secured and in position

we swung the bikes out of the field and went back down to the beach to prepare our afternoon meal. Wullicks and limpets were on the menu. Wullicks had a variety of names including: willicks, welks, periwinkles, winkles and sea-snails and they were as plentiful as their names. Limpets always had a vice-like grip on the rocks and they needed to be thumped with a stone to prise them off. They were still commonly collected and eaten by townsfolk, and were usually cooked by coating them in oat-meal and frying them in butter. Today they were being boiled, in a tin can of sea-water, on an open fire. They came to the boil fairly quickly and the pin was passed around to tease the wullicks and limpets hot from their shells. In France, they are considered a delicacy, but they couldn't have tasted any better than those cooked fresh on the shores of Strangford Lough.

...

The next day mirrored the one before. Some kids found the monotony of the long summer days' boring. We never did. There was a simple question: would you rather be messing around town with your mates or at school? There was only one answer which trumped any thoughts of boredom.

We met in the football field and then called at Maggie's to finish her garden. The same tools were produced and we set to with renewed vigour. The long grass was now in retreat, and with the end in sight, it encouraged us to quicken our pace to complete the task. With the grass cut, raked and bagged, we took a well-earned rest on the summer-seat, as before. Maggie, obviously waiting for that moment came out with the lemonade and biscuits. This time, there were ice-cubes in the glasses, we were right, she did have a fridge. Turbo picked up where he had left off and continued chatting her up.

"We were out Bankmore swimming yesterday, Maggie."

"Oh, were ye now?" replied Maggie. "Aye, and an oul' farmer tried to steal Finn's underpants!"

"I hope ye weren't wearing them at the time," said Maggie to Finn.

This was the first time that Maggie had said anything remotely amusing and it was funnier because of that. Turbo's magic was beginning to work and perhaps he was right that 'she wasn't such a bad oul' spud' after all.

"No, I got them back," said Finn.

"We called in with JP for a water-break," said Turbo, "he gets his water from an old well and it's as cold as these ice-bergs."

"Cubes," corrected Finn, as Turbo continued.

"He was very pleased that we were helping ye in the garden. Always has a great word on ye. Margaret was the Sunday in every week, I think they were his very words."

"Oh, were they now?" I could see Maggie

twiddling with her hair again but, whereas, you could read JP's face like a book, Maggie's was a blank page.

This long range courtship continued for some weeks with us boys carrying the chat, which wasn't chat but was thought to be chat, between Burn Brae and Bankmore. We cut Maggie's hedges, dug out flower beds, gave the grass another whack when it threatened to grow back, anything really to keep the lines of communication open.

Other than Maggie having the neatest garden in her row we didn't seem to be making any noticeable progress. As we were inexperienced at matchmaking, and inexperienced at everything else as well, we had no idea how to reach the 'lived happily ever after' stage. Then, just as we were about to give up, the answer presented itself right in front of us, at the Orange Hall. There was a notice on the gate advertising an Old Time Dance in the hall on Saturday night, this was the break-through we had been hoping for. Finn wisely advised that it would be inappropriate for Maggie to ask JP as it was the man's place to ask the lady. With that in mind we were off to JP's to lay the ground work.

On the way we called into my grandmothers to see if she needed water, she didn't but our thoughtfulness brought us a tanner each. Now money didn't exactly burn a hole in our pockets but, for whatever reason, it didn't stay there very long either. We made it the short distance to Cook Street where there was the last sweetie shop heading out of town in that direction.

We bought three Sherbet Dabs, I am not sure why we did, as it was a sweet that caused as much pain as pleasure. They consisted of a cardboard tube which was filled with a yellow, fizzy acidic powder and a stick of licorice. The idea was to lick the licorice and dab it in the powder, in a controlled manner, and eat the contents in that way. Being boys who liked to live dangerously, the licorice was always eaten first, and the contents poured straight into the mouth. This caused something of an internal explosion followed by a fit of coughing, sputtering and watering of eyes. The buzz of the fizzy powder was only beginning to clear our heads when JP's cottage came into view.

As usual we went round the side of the house and found JP in the vegetable garden. We liked helping JP in the garden as it largely consisted of sitting on a log watching him work and giving him a bit of horticultural advice here and there. At times we were asked to fetch something or other and that probably was the extent of our usefulness. JP was digging up some new potatoes.

"What variety are they?" asked Finn.

"Dublin Queens!"

"How could they be Dublin Queens when Dublin doesn't have a Queen?"

"Well, ye don't expect a good Irish man, like myself, to be consorting with British Queens now, do ye Finn?"

"No, but I bet ye they're all the same."

"Aye, maybe yer right."

This raised a doubt whether such a good Irish man would consort with an Orange Hall, but Turbo opened the discussion.

"I see there's an old time dance in the Orange Hall on Saturday night," said Turbo.

"By Jaysus, the Hooley in the Hall, it was always the best dance of the year." JP's response immediately dispelled our doubts.

"You've been there before, then," said Finn.

"Ach aye, mind you what ye'll always see is young bucks who would normally face a lion petrified to ask a girl to dance."

"They line up on one side of the hall and the girls on the other. Ye would think the gulf between them was the deepest part of Strangford Lough."

"What are they afraid of?" asked Finn

"Refusal. They're afraid of making the crossing but having to return without a passenger. However, as the night goes on they eventually summon up the courage."

"So, there's drink at it then?"

"Oh no, it's the same as the Parochial Hall, no drink in the Hall and dancing stops at 12.00pm sharp, so that there's no dancing on the Sabbath."

"While there's no drink in the Hall that doesn't mean there's no drink in the men. Many arrive from the pub or they use one of these," JP produced a silver hip flask from his back pocket.

"Even if it was the deepest part of the Lough, a drop or two of whiskey soon has the feet walking and mouth talking!"

"Maggie was saying that she used to love all the old time dances," said Turbo casually.

"Indeed she did, and she could shake a leg with the best of them," we found that hard to believe, but JP continued.

"She never refused anyone a dance and she was never aff the flure."

"Aye, she was saying that she would love to give it another go before she gets too old to shake a leg, " said Turbo, delivering his knock-out punch.

"Ye know what, so would I," said JP, "tell her if she wants a birl round the flure, well I'm her man!" JP was again beaming from ear to ear.

We left JP's punching the air, until Finn reminded us, that Maggie had expressed no interest at all of going to a dance.

"Ah, don't worry about that," said Turbo confidently, "just leave Maggie to me!"

So, we did just that, and went straight from JP's without distraction or short-cuts, to Maggie's front door. As usual, she opened it quickly on the first rap.

"I don't think I need anything done in the garden this week," she said, when she saw us on the door-step.

"We're not here to do gardening," said Turbo, "we've a message from JP."

"Well come in for a minute, but be quick, as I'm on my way out."

"JP was saying that there's an old time dance in the

Orange Hall on Saturday night, and back in the day, you were a great one for the dancing."

"Back in the day, indeed!" said Maggie.

"Aye, he said if ye would go with him that youse could still show the young 'uns a thing or two."

"Did he now?" We stood waiting for an answer but there was none forthcoming, ignoring the awkward silence, Turbo continued.

"Well, will I tell him that ye'll go, then?"

"Tell him that I'll think about it." With that we were bundled out and Maggie went on about her business. It wasn't the outcome we had been hoping for and we certainly weren't going out to Bankmore just to say she was thinking about it. Finn offered a glimmer of hope pointing out that at least she didn't say 'No' outright.

During the course of the day we weighed up the chances of Maggie saying 'Yes' and our hopes varied from optimism to despondency. When we analysed it closely, it was clear that Maggie had never said anything nice about JP, we were almost believing what we had told him. Any compliments from JP, which usually he hadn't said either, were often met with nothing more than 'Oh, did he now?' But, it was an answer rather than a question that we were looking for, when we arrived at Maggie's door the next morning.

"We're going out to Bankmore swimming today Maggie," said Turbo, "have ye thought about what we were saying yesterday?"

"Aye, tell him there's no fool like an oul' fool," our hearts immediately sank but she continued.

"He can pick me up here at nine o'clock on Saturday night. I'm not standing outside Toner's waiting on him."

She quickly closed the door and we hardly stopped running until we arrived at JP's cottage. He was delighted with the news.

"By Jaysus, I better get the dancing shoes out and get a bit of practice in!"

He slapped his thighs with enthusiasm and did a bit of a jig on the scullery floor. We joined in and only hoped that he could dance better on Saturday night.

"Here, don't spend all that in the one shop," said JP, as he put a half-crown into Turbo's hand.

An hour or so later we were sipping brown lemonade in Teenie's shop with the intention of also trying the brandy balls and wine-gums. We were more than happy with our success as matchmakers but if there ever was a next time we would be looking for two people in the same street rather than two miles apart. Still, the miles we had put in over the summer seemed to make it even more satisfying.

"Well, any craic with yis, today?" said Teenie, which was better than asking what we had for breakfast.

"Aye, we've been matchmaking," said Finn.

"Matchmaking? And who have ye been making a match between?" said Teenie laughing.

"John Pat Murphy and Maggie Mason. He's taking her to the dance in the Orange Hall on Saturday night."

"Are ye serious?" said Teenie, not knowing whether to believe us or not.

Finn briefly outlined the story so far as we drank up and made to leave the shop. Teenie produced the bottle of lemonade from below the counter.

"Here, ye may as well finish that off, there's hardly a glass in it," and she topped up our glasses.

It was, of course, a delaying tactic until she got the full story, about what he said, what she said and what we said. News, gossip and scandal of any description was a valuable commodity in a small town and old women were the main hunter-gatherers and traders in such a commodity. They were never slow to add in their own tuppence-worth and that investment could quickly increase to sixpence or a shilling's worth in the retelling. Only when Teenie was satisfied, that she had properly discharged her duty of obtaining all relevant information, were we free to leave.

Just outside the door Dickie Doran was standing talking to someone, but we managed to slip past without being seen, and Blackie confined himself to wagging his tail rather than barking and giving us away. Dickie would be Teenie's first customer after we left and, no doubt, would be told about JP and Maggie. The next person that Dickie met would then also be told and so on. By the time we walked around the town, we would inevitably meet the story coming down Church Street, in much the same way as the McNabb story met us on the shore-front on the morning after the incident. For now, we strolled across to the Orange Hall for another look at the poster advertising the Old Time Dance, just to be sure that we had got the facts right, thankfully we had.

Saturday evening arrived and we took up our monitoring positions beneath the two big chestnut trees opposite the Police Station. It was a prime location as we had a clear view of Anne Street, Church Street and Burn Brae. At the expected time JP appeared at the top of Anne Street. As he got closer Finn whispered,

"I think he has splashed out on a new pair of braces."

Indeed, he was sporting a wine-coloured pair of braces that matched the colour of his tie and they were well set off against an immaculate white shirt. He wore his best dark suit and hat which he doffed to two ladies standing chatting at their front doors. They continued to watch him as he passed with arms-folded and tongues-wagging, they were no doubt aware of where he was going. He was carrying a small box of chocolates which, in itself, may have betrayed his mission if he had been trying to keep it secret.. He had the walk of a happy man as he stepped up and knocked Maggie's door.

Maggie didn't answer the door quite as quickly as she did when she knew it was us boys after a ball. JP shuffled from one foot to the other until the door opened and he went inside. When they re-emerged, Maggie was wearing a blue summer frock that seemed to come blinking out into the light as it probably hadn't seen the evening sunshine for long many a year. She had got her hair done, whatever that entailed, and had put on some make-up. They were a very presentable couple as they made their way up Church Street towards the Orange Hall.

We gave them enough time to make it to the Orange Hall before following in their footsteps up Church Street. At The Square we could hear the rise and fall of the music as the door of the Orange Hall opened and closed. On closer inspection we could see the scene that JP had so accurately described. Along one side of the Hall were young men talking and laughing nervously, while smoking cigarettes. Opposite them young girls were sitting on benches furtively eyeing up the young men, occasionally, allowing eye-contact with the one they hoped would make the treacherous crossing to pick them for a dance. There were a number of couples on the floor, as this was the best time to dance when there was plenty of space, but we couldn't see Maggie or JP.

As there was really nothing to see we decided to take a stroll down Ferry Street. If there was nothing to see at the Orange Hall it was happening at Dumigan's and the Slip Inn. They were packed to the doors with noise, laughter and singing spilling out on to the street. The big orange sun was taking its evening dip in the Lough which seemed to set the water on fire and the ferry boat looked as if it was entering and emerging from an inferno. We sat and watched the sunset for a short time and then made our way back up the Shambles to the Orange Hall. In the time it took us to walk around the block it had all kicked-off. The pubs and hip flasks had emptied and the place was jumping this was the Hooley in the Hall in action. And jumping was a more accurate description than dancing!

The band was made up of a few ceilidh band players and some Orange Band musicians; they had toiled now for more than an hour to get the crowd to their feet. Unlike the professional Show Bands, that played the Locarno Ballroom, they had a limited repertoire and for a bit of a break they were now calling singers from the floor. On the way up the Shambles, I thought I had heard the strains of Do Wah Diddy Diddy, but I couldn't say for certain that Diddy Diddy was in town. Unsurprisingly, JP was called on for a song and we could see him making his way to the stage and talking to the band-leader. A hush fell on the crowd, surely he was not going to sing the Irish Republican ballad Kevin Barry, in an Orange Hall? He took the microphone and announced, "This is a song about the Windmill Hill," but it wasn't:-

"I wandered today to the hills, Maggie
To watch the scene below
The creek and the creaking old mill, Maggie

As we used to long, long ago

The green grove has gone from the hills, Maggie
Where first the daisies sprung
The creaking old mill is still, Maggie
Since you and I were young

Oh, they say that I'm feeble with age, Maggie
My steps are much slower than then
My face is a well written page, Maggie
And time all alone was the pen

They say that we have outlived our time, Maggie
As dated the song that we've sung
But to me you're as fair as you were, Maggie
When you and I were young

They say we have outlived our time, Maggie
As dated the song that we've sung
But to me you're as fair as you were, Maggie
When you and I were young
When you and I were young."

There was only one person in the Hall who had
ever heard JP sing that song before and she had a tear
in her eye. She squeezed his hand, as he returned
from the stage, with the applause still ringing out. JP
had played his trump card, the Ace of Hearts, and he
had won the heart of Maggie. The dance broke up on
the stroke of midnight with someone thanking the

band and the crowd. JP and Maggie walked back up Church Street arm and arm and we followed the crowd back home by High Street. Mission accomplished or so we thought.

PART III

THE TIDE TURNS

After the Hooley in the Hall it was widely acknowledged about town that JP and Maggie were 'walking out'. We thought this was a compulsory part of courtship as a Sunday didn't pass that they weren't seen walking round by the chapel or along the Walter Shore, out Bankmore or up the Mountain Road, always returning to Maggie's for tea in the evening. They were enjoying the autumn of their years and the summer was also beginning to slip imperceptibly into that season.

Farmers were still making hay while the sun shone, and tractors pulling cartloads of rickety bales were a common sight on the country roads. Flocks of crows and pigeons picked over the stubble, birds and animals everywhere were preparing for the lean months ahead. JP's soup vegetables were growing away strongly and would be ready when the time came. There was a melancholy mood in the air and the first thoughts of returning to school started to surface. The last of the summer swimming was fast approaching, when the swimming gear was packed away at the end of summer it would not be seen again until the following June. The first of the big harvest moons were beginning to bathe the fields in its soft mellow light as activity on farms began to slow and the land fell silent.

JP had been busy helping various farmers and more often than not there was no smoke rising from the chimney. On one of our last swimming excursions of the year we found him sitting at the back of the house polishing a pair of black shoes. He was in a pensive mood.

"I'm going up to see the PP this evening," he said, giving the shoes another shine, "mind you, I haven't always seen eye to eye with the clergy."

"What's it about, JP?" asked Turbo.

"It's about getting married."

"And do we know the lucky girl?" laughed Finn and JP smiled.

"What's the new PP like?"

"Father Magee is great with all the altar boys and anyone who's met him has a good word on him," said Turbo reassuringly.

Still, JP seemed ill at ease about meeting the new parish priest, and so we left him to his shoes and thoughts.

When the appointed time came JP swung his bicycle out onto the road and began cycling towards the town. It was a cool summer evening and as he was in no hurry he enjoyed a leisurely cycle to Cook

Street and up the Chapel Turn towards the Parochial House. He parked his bicycle against the graveyard wall and took the hip-flask from his back pocket. He took a couple of sips and popped a Polo Mint into his mouth. After waiting until there was a sufficient minty flavour to his breath he went up and knocked the door.

At that time there was no appointment system you simply went to the Parochial House and asked 'is the priest at home?' If a mass-murderer had arrived just before you, and was determined to tell the priest all his misdemeanors, you had to wait until he had finished or go home and come back sometime again.

The priest's housekeeper, Minnie McGrattan, answered the door. Minnie ran the Parochial House and its incumbent with great efficiency. In many ways she was the power behind the throne and in effect ran the Parish. She told the PP what he needed to remember, what he shouldn't forget, who he should meet, where he needed to be and at what time, all without ever writing anything down. She had witnessed all the religious ceremonies in the Parish for the past fifty years and was an authority on how things should be done. She was also on very friendly terms with the bishop, and knew he liked a nice bit of white fish with floury potatoes and peas, after he conducted the confirmation ceremony in May.

If you were looking for a cure for 'warts, farts or broken hearts' this was the woman to speak to, but she was also the woman who would chase any such person from the door, without hesitating to emphasize her point with the floor brush. As housekeeper, cook and secretary she was invaluable to a new PP like Father Magee.

JP removed his hat, and said, "Is He in residence?"

"Indeed, he is John Pat. Come in, he's in his study I'll let him know he has a visitor."

JP was shown into an interior room. There was a quietness and stillness about it with a smell of candle-wax. It was dimly lit except for a flickering red light below a picture of the Sacred Heart, on the opposite wall was a crucifix and the grave ticking of a pendulum clock seemed to be life itself ticking away, in reality it was. A statue of the Child of Prague, looked forlornly out of a small window, at the dwindling summer light as it contemplated the daunting prospect of the task ahead.

In the centre of the room was a long, polished rectangular table with four red velvet covered chairs and similar chairs placed against the wall at intervals around the room. At the head of the table was a writing-pad and pen, JP correctly assumed that this was the PP's seat, so he sat on the chair positioned half-way down the length of the table. With the amplified ticking of the clock he was thinking that it was like a giant confessional-box. He imagined that if the mass-murderer had been in before him that he would have slumped to his knees and told all.

With such thoughts the opening of the door startled him as Father Magee breezed in and shook hands across the table. He was young for a PP, and his pleasantness outweighed the gravitas that priests in general, and PPs in particular, liked to carry around with them.

"John Pat, isn't it? I don't think we've met. I haven't got round everyone yet."

"No, I'm sure ye haven't reached the wilds of Bankmore as yet. How are ye settling in?"

"It's grand, after mass in the morning I walk up the Windmill Hill and watch the Lough flowing by. It's God's own country here, I never want to go back to Belfast, that's for sure!"

"And, Mrs. McGrattan, she's a God-send. If the Pope knew about her she would be running the Vatican. When I come down from the Mount, so to speak, she has the bacon and eggs on the table."

"Except for Fridays," quipped JP, warming to Father Magee's bonhomie.

"Sure, with the big fat herrings you get in this part of the country, I could eat them all week."

"Anyway, how can I help you?" said Father Magee sitting down in front of the writing-pad and taking up the pen.

"I'm looking to get married," said JP.

"And do you know a girl who's looking in the same direction?"

"Yes, Margaret Mason." Father Magee started to write on the note-pad.

"John Patrick Murphy, I presume."

"Yes, that's what I was christened, though I'm

now called a few other things as well."

"And Margaret Mason. Both Catholics?"

"No, Margaret has no religion. She married her first husband in the Church of Ireland but never followed that religion thereafter."

"She's agnostic then?"

"If that's the word on it."

Father Magee put down his pen and for the first time looked rather serious.

"I'm afraid I can't marry you in the chapel unless you are both Catholic. The bishop wouldn't allow it. Do you think Margaret would turn Catholic?"

"I dunno, we've never talked about religion. What would she have to do?"

"Well, she would need to learn the various prayers and know the sacraments of the church. If I was satisfied that she did then she could be baptised and you could get married. Mind you, I wouldn't be too hard on her, we need all the recruits we can get!" said Father Magee, trying to restore some levity.

"Why don't you ask her and see how the land lies and we can take it from there."

"I will," said JP, who was rather crestfallen but fully appreciating that Father Magee had no discretion in the matter.

"And I should point out," continued Father Magee, "that any children of the marriage have to be brought up as Catholic."

"By Jaysus Father, forgive me for taking the Lord's name in vain, but sure neither of us would tear in the plucking!"

"Well, the Lord works in mysterious ways," said Father Magee, "and I have to advise you about all your responsibilities."

JP was rather perplexed at the prospect of such a mysterious happening when Father Magee burst out laughing.

"I'm only joking you!" He was even more perplexed at a PP joking about such matters. They got up from the table and shook hands again and Mrs. McGrattan arrived to show JP to the door.

It was now dusk as he walked over to the graveyard wall. He had another sip from his hip flask, gave a deep sigh, as he flicked the light on his bike and rode slowly towards Burn Brae processing his thoughts on the way. At the brow of Ballyphilip Hill he pressed down hard on the pedals and free-wheeled almost to St Columba's School. From High Street he again free-wheeled down Anne Street and into Burn Brae. Maggie answered the door fairly quickly as she had been expecting him.

He related how the events at the Parochial House had unfolded, mostly looking at his polished shoes as he spoke, and occasionally glancing at Maggie's face to see how she was receiving the news.

"Yer forgetting that I'm from England and we don't eat and sleep religion like youse do here. The way youse talk about Catholics and Protestants ye wouldn't think ye were all part of the same religion!"

"Didn't I marry Thomas in the Church of Ireland

and I've no problem doing what needs to be done to marry you in the chapel. I don't want to go off to Belfast or somewhere else to get married."

JP was greatly relieved, "I'll let Minnie McGrattan know and she'll tell the PP. One thing about Minnie, everything that goes on in the Parochial House stays there, and is never gossiped about the town."

As JP was leaving we were making it home before dark, as instructed, well actually it was after dark but we tended to push the boundaries.

"Hey, Turbo will yis give me a shout tomorrow. I can't talk now as I need a drink before Toner's close."

We wondered how he had got on with Father Magee but he seemed to be in a better mood at any rate.

Next morning, we got the bikes out and were travelling in formation along the Shore with Big Bertha flanked on either side by Finn and Turbo. Finn kept up a running commentary as we shot down enemy aircraft flying low over Strangford Lough. Eventually, with their mission completed the spitfires landed at JP's.

"Ah, it's the three wise men," said JP, in his usual happy manner.

"Well, did he agree to marry yis?" said Finn.

"He nearly did but Maggie needs to turn Catholic before we can get married in the chapel."

"Is she a Protestant, then?" asked Turbo.

"No, she's agnostic."

"Well, she must be a Protestant agnostic if she

needs to become a Catholic."

"She must be," said JP, not wishing to get into a theological discussion.

"The thing is, she needs to learn the Catholic prayers and all about the sacraments and I thought you boys could teach her."

"Haven't youse been altar boys for years and served at baptisms, marriages, funerals and bar mitzvahs."

We couldn't remember any bar mitzvahs but it was a minor detail. We had become altar boys some years earlier. Our mothers took great pride in washing, ironing and starching our surplices and soutanes which was the required attire for all altar boys at the time. They felt sure that the next step was the priesthood only for their hopes to be dashed when a letter arrived home informing them that we had been caught drinking the altar wine. Our defence of 'waste not want not' fell on deaf ears.

For each mass two cruets of wine and water, were set out for the priest conducting the mass. The curate preferred mostly wine with a small drop of water and the old PP mostly water and a small drop of wine. As a result, the remaining wine was washed done the sink in the vestry. We thought rather than waste it that we should drink it. Really it was like sugared water and not half as good or refreshing as brown lemonade. This went on for some time until we were eventually caught in the act by the PP. He was generally a cross man, and particularly cross on this occasion, hence the very stern letters that arrived home threatening us with dismissal. We would have been happy enough to accept dismissal, as it seemed to be an organisation that we had somehow got ourselves into, but had no idea how to get out of it.

In the beginning everything was new and exciting. As you entered the vestry at St. Patrick's chapel the bell-rope hung very invitingly. How we managed to resist the temptation to swing on it only the Lord himself knows. John Joe who rang the bell, at times, let us have a go under his very strict supervision. The novelty soon wore off when we had to get up at six o'clock in the morning to serve the early mass in the small oratory, in the Parochial Hall at the Shore. When we arrived at the Hall we had to sit on the stairs until the curate arrived to turn on all the lights and unlock the vestry which was a cubby-hole under the stairs. The stair-case and all the floors in the building were made of wood which creaked and groaned in the silence. Some altar boys swore that they sometimes heard foot-steps on the wooden floor just above. Sitting in the gloom listening to the old building talking to itself often had the heart thumping and I always preferred to wait outside, whatever the weather, until the first mass-goers arrived. It was a huge relief when the new St. Cooey's oratory in The Square was built.

The highlight of the altar boy year was the annual outing. Any tips we got for serving at weddings or funerals would go into a general fund so it was really a trip we funded ourselves. It would be something like a trip to Strule Wells in Downpatrick for a picnic, singing Hail Glorious Saint Patrick, all the way there and back. We were beginning to find it increasingly difficult to 'bestow a sweet smile' and to say that we were becoming disenchanted with it all would be a fair comment.

"Hey JP, why don't ye teach her yerself," said Finn, "sure yer a Catholic."

"Well, ye see, I think I've forgotten more than I used to know, as I don't attend anymore."

"Sure, we see ye at the chapel most Sundays," continued Finn.

"I'm what ye might call a back-door Catholic. I cycle up to the chapel just as mass is ending, it takes the bad look off me, and stops people talking."

"I fell out with the old PP many years ago, it was over Margaret's first husband Thomas," JP's voice began to falter and hesitatingly, he said, "you see, I killed him!"

He took out his handkerchief and wiped his face and eyes. We had never seen a man cry before, and were unsure what to do, so we just sat there and stared in silence until JP recovered sufficiently to continue.

"It was an accident, of course."

We were much relieved to hear that, matchmaking was proving difficult enough but crime-investigators may just have been beyond us.

"It was a winter's night and we were getting reddup around the yard. I was reversing the tractor, and in the dark and rain, I didn't see Thomas and he didn't hear me as he came round the corner. He struck his head on the concrete and was dead before the doctor arrived from the town."

"At the time the mother and I were living in the town. After a while there were rumours going about that I had deliberately killed Thomas because he married Margaret. I would hardly have continued working for them if that had been the case."

"Anyway, I decided to go and talk it over with the PP, I remember it was a Friday night. The PP himself came to the door, and before I could explain myself, he said that whatever I had to say I could say in confession. I told him that it was not about sinfulness and, therefore, I had nothing to tell him in confession. One word led to another and we fell out, I think I must have been keeping him from his steak and chips!"

This was a stinging remark from JP, we thought a priest shouldn't even be enjoying chips on a fast day, never mind steak.

"To escape the whispering and talk going on behind my back, me and the mother moved out here. She didn't see her old friends as often and it broke her heart. She went to her grave earlier than she should have."

JP again wiped his face with his handkerchief and we could feel tears stinging in our eyes as we forced them to stay there.

"Anyway, short story long, that's why I'm asking yis to teach Maggie what she needs to know to become a Catholic. Will ye do it?"

"Sure, we will!" said Turbo glad to be able to strike an upbeat note.

. . .

Arrangements were made with Maggie for us to call, on two evenings the following week for her Catholic instruction. We decided among ourselves that Finn was best suited to this task. Finn, in turn, decided that on the first evening he would cover sins and sacraments and all the Catholic prayers on the second evening.

The nights were beginning to draw in and getting colder. When we arrived on the Monday evening Maggie had the fire blazing away. As we sat down around the fire Maggie brought a plate of toast and three cups of tea from the kitchen. With the tea and toast quickly accounted for Finn started with the seven sacraments. Maggie had a note-book and pen ready and sat at a small table scribbling down whatever she thought was useful.

Finn explained that there were seven Catholic sacraments: baptism, confession, communion, confirmation, matrimony, anointing the sick and Holy Orders.

"Because yer getting married Maggie, ye can forget about the Holy Orders and probably anointing of the sick until yer dying. The first thing you will need to do is to get baptised. The PP will say a few words and pour holy water on yer head."

"Will he soak my hair," asked Maggie with some concern.

"Well, I don't know about that," said Turbo, "as we have only seen babies being baptised and they usually have no hair. But I'm sure it's not going to be a shampoo and blow dry!"

I am not sure how much this reassured Maggie, but Finn continued to explain all the sacraments in turn, with Maggie writing away.

"And then there's the seven deadly sins, pride, greed, wrath, envy, lust, gluttony and sloth," said Finn getting into full flow.

"The magnificent seven, Maggie!" added Turbo. "God's on the side of the sacraments and the Devil's on the side of the sins."

"I think the Devil probably has more fun," said Maggie, without lifting her head from her writing.

"If you commit any of those sins you go straight to Hell as they are mortal sins," continued Finn, "smaller sins are called venial sins and if ye commit any of those ye might have to go to Purgatory before being allowed into Heaven."

"Well, I think that's enough for tonight boys, I'll learn what I've written down and I'll see yis on Wednesday night."

When we arrived on the Wednesday evening Maggie had the tea and toast already made. As we munched our way through the toast, Maggie recited what she had learned on Monday night and she was word perfect. Very satisfied with the progress Finn started with the prayers.

"D'ye want to learn them in Latin or English, Maggie?" asked Finn.

We actually did know some Latin as we had become altar boys just as the Latin mass was being phased out. Most of the time we didn't actually know what we were saying but we liked the rhythm and incantation of it. There was one old man who always sat in the front seat of the chapel and you never heard his word during the mass in English. But when it came to the Latin mass he rose to the occasion and was heard above everyone else. We thought that he was either a Latin scholar or was once an altar boy and knew how terrifying it was for young boys to get all the Latin responses right.

"I think English would be fine," said Maggie.

The process took a lot longer than the first night. Finn slowly recited the various prayers and Maggie wrote then down word for word. The Apostles Creed, Our Father, Glory Be, Act of Contrition, when it came to the Confiteor, Finn insisted on including the Latin phrase 'mea culpa, mea culpa, mea maxima culpa (through my fault, through my fault, through my most grievous fault), as most priests preferred this version and so did he.

He then went on to explain the Rosary with five decades each containing ten Hail Marys.

"I hope the Hail Marys aren't long," said Maggie.

"No they're not," replied Finn. "but I'll leave Turbo to finish it, as my aunt calls on a Wednesday evening and she likes to give me a shilling or two. I wouldn't want to disappoint her."

With that Finn made for the door and Turbo took over. Maggie was again busy writing as Turbo slowly recited the Hail Mary.

"Hail Mary full of grace,
The Lord is with thee,
Blessed art thou amongst women,
And blessed is the fruit of thy womb Jesus,
Holy Mary mother of God,
Send us down a couple of bob,
Pray for us sinners,
Now and at the hour of our death.
Amen."

"I bet ye Finn's saying that one all the way home to see the aunt," said Maggie, smiling to herself as she finished the writing.

"Another thing that's useful to know Maggie is that Mary appeared twice in Ireland. At Knock in County Mayo and down the Virgin's Lane at Cuan Place. If Father Magee asks ye to say the Hail Mary he would be very impressed if you also mentioned that fact."

"Well, thank God that's all for tonight. No wonder I never bothered much with religion," said Maggie looking over the pages of prayers that she had written down.

"Do ye want us to come back to test ye on them, Maggie," I asked.

"No, once I have them written down I can learn them quickly enough."

Maggie showed us out and we went running down the street.

" I hope the Big Lady sends Finn down a couple of bob from the aunt," said Turbo, as we continued running and laughing down the street.

Maggie was a fast learner and she was confident enough to meet with the PP the following week. If everything went well there would be a short baptismal ceremony in the Parochial House. JP cycled in from Bankmore, and they enjoyed the stroll out to the chapel in the autumn sunshine, as the year slowly ebbed away.

Mrs. McGrattan welcomed them at the door and they were shown into the same room that JP had been in before. Father Magee entered shortly after and was introduced to Maggie. He put everyone quickly at their ease.

"I'll do mum," he said, as he poured the tea that Mrs. McGrattan had brought in and passed around a plate of biscuits. There were no Marie biscuits or even custard creams here, it was thick, butter short-bread that Minnie had made. JP could have eaten the whole plateful but managed to restrain himself, Maggie being a little nervous only took the tea.

With formalities over Father Magee went over the same topics that we had covered with Maggie, with perhaps a slightly better grasp of the detail. He was very impressed with her knowledge, particularly, with her 'mea culpa', Finn was right on that one. He then explained the significance of the Rosary in the Catholic faith and asked Maggie to finish with the Hail Mary, which she did.

"Hail Mary full of grace,
The Lord is with thee,
Blessed art thou amongst women,
And blessed is the fruit of thy womb Jesus,
Holy Mary mother of God,
Send us down a couple of bob,
Pray for us sinners,
Now and at the hour of our death.
Amen."

There was immediate panic in JP's face but Maggie was in full flow and there was no stopping her.

"I also believe that the Blessed Virgin appeared twice in Ireland, at Knock in County Mayo and down Cuan Place which is also known as the Virgin's Lane."

JP looked alarmingly at Father Magee but the PP only burst out laughing and JP joined in from relief more than anything else. Maggie was rather disconcerted with this reaction as she knew she was word perfect. When Father Magee recovered his composure he gently pointed out the slight discrepancies.

"That Turbot will be getting fried when I get a hold of him!" exclaimed Maggie, but in the end she saw the funny side of it.

JP was thinking that the old PP would never have seen the funny side of it, he rarely saw the funny side of anything and his thoughts wandered to a very different Friday night at the Parochial House many years ago. With Maggie's baptism completed, they saw no need to delay proceedings, and the wedding was set for Wednesday fortnight. Mrs. McGrattan arrived to show them to the door.

"Mrs. McGrattan what do you think of our altar boys telling poor Mrs. Mason that the Blessed Virgin had appeared down Cuan Place?"

"Well, how do ye know she didn't, isn't it called the Virgin's Lane?"

JP could tell from this short exchange that these two got on like a house on fire and that the Parish was in safe hands.

"Mrs. McGrattan, that short-bread was beautiful, you must give Margaret the recipe as I would like to be kept in the manner to which I have become accustomed," he said smiling.

Minnie was delighted with that remark. She was used to visiting priests and others taking such things for granted and never being thankful for small mercies. It was a trait that Maggie found endearing about John Pat, he was always gentlemanly and went out of his way to thank people. As the door of the

Parochial House closed, the door to their new life together opened, and there was an extra spring in their step as they made for home.

Next morning, we called at Maggie's to see how they had got on. Luckily for Turbo perhaps, she was out so we decided to go out to JP's, it was only four miles there and back after all. We found JP sitting in the living room.

"Well, how did it go?" said Finn.

"It was going very well," said JP dejectedly, "until we got to the Hail Mary."

"Turbo, you did the Hail Mary," said Finn.

"Jeesus, I forgot to tell her to take the funny bit out of it. I thought we were going back to test her on it and I would have told her then."

"Well," continued JP in the same downbeat manner, "we may have got away with the Hail Mary but, by Jaysus, didn't Maggie tell the PP that the Blessed Virgin had appeared down the Virgin's Lane."

"Jeesus, I forgot about that as well!" said Turbo, quite disturbed at the thought that he had ruined everything.

"Now do ye want the goods news or the bad news?" asked JP.

"I think we could do with some good news," replied Finn rather seriously.

"I'm only joking, it went well and we're getting married Wednesday fortnight! The bad news is that Father Magee has agreed to you three serving at the wedding but yis will have to get the day off school."

We were all dancing around the living room endangering JP's mother's antique dresser, with the day off school being celebrated as much as the forthcoming wedding.

"We're going for a feed in the Hotel afterwards and yer mothers are also invited so make sure ye tell them."

JP then produced three pound notes and gave us a pound each.

"I know what I give ye at the wedding will go into the altar boy fund so that's for yerselves."

We were speechless, which was something of a rarity, we only ever traded in coins and usually of a low denomination at that. Each of us gave the pound to our mothers and told them about the wedding invite. There was an immediate flurry about having nothing to wear, which we ignored, as we knew cometh the day they would all be out in their finery.

...

And the day arrived quickly enough. In the interval Maggie had been to Newtownards and had bought herself a new outfit complete with matching shoes, hat and handbag. The two witnesses to the wedding, were to be Maggie's neighbours of nearly thirty years, wee Mr. and Mrs. Tomelty. The Tomeltys had raised a big family of boys and had a fairly relaxed attitude to footballs being kicked into their garden. They either took the view that, boys will be boys and they'll grow up soon enough, or that Maggie was more than capable of fighting the battle by herself, which she was. It was the morning of the wedding and the car had just arrived to take them to the chapel.

Meanwhile JP was already there sitting in the front pew. The Latin scholar had been relegated to the next seat behind JP but his services would not be required today at any rate. The usual mass-goers had taken up their positions as had our mothers near the front of the chapel. JP had also bought a new dark suit and was looking very dapper.

"He's giving the red-braces another run out," reported Finn, as he returned to the sacristy after lighting the candles. Father Magee went out and checked that everything was in order. He went over to JP and whispered,

"I hope she's not going to keep you waiting."

"Sure, I've been waiting for nearly forty years and a few more minutes won't matter," said JP calmly.

And with that, the wedding party arrived and took up their seats beside him. The wedding ceremony passed off smoothly as it always did. We always waited, in anticipation, when the priest said:-

"If any person knows why this man and woman should not be joined in Holy Matrimony, let them speak now or forever hold their peace."

In the movies someone always burst in at that point to great dramatic effect, which we always hoped would happen but it never did. Other than a baby crying at the back of the church there were no objections and Maggie and JP were wed.

When mass was over the married couple came into the vestry to sign the register, along with Mr. and Mrs. Tomelty, and arrangements were made to go to the Hotel. Maggie and JP went on ahead in the wedding car, Father Magee took himself and the Tomeltys in his car and we walked round by the shore with our mothers. This was our first time ever in the Hotel and JP was at the door to show us where to go. The others were already seated at a long table which dazzled with an array of cutlery, glasses and plates.

"Well ladies and gentlemen, what will yis have to drink?" asked JP in his usual affable style. Our mothers had a glass of white wine each and we had brown lemonade. "There's plenty more where that came from boys," said JP, winking at us.

The first course on the menu was prawn-cocktails, to be followed by turkey and ham, sherry trifle with tea and coffee to finish. When the first course arrived Father Magee stood up to say Grace and a few encouraging words about the married couple. JP got up to respond, we hoped he wouldn't take long, as we had never tasted prawn-cocktails before and they looked really appetizing. We hadn't heard anything he said until he mentioned us.

"I always call these three, the three wise men, and they're a lot smarter than they look, although their mothers have them looking particularly smart today. But without them none of us would be sitting here today."

He then proposed a toast to our health and future happiness. Our mothers swelled with pride at someone saying something nice about us for a change, and in front of the PP, hopes of the priesthood were perhaps on the rise again. Our only hope was to get stuck into the prawn-cocktails, as soon as possible, which we did immediately JP made to sit down.

The lemonade was topped up a few times, we could eat as much as we wanted and did, an extra helping of sherry trifle was called for to complete the feast. Over tea and coffee Mr. Tomelty was explaining some local history to Father Magee, and with five ladies and a story-teller together, the conversation never ceased. Eventually, with tea nearly finished JP was called on for a song.

"This song is for my mother," he said, and he sang Kevin Barry, and then he said, "this one's for my wife although Father Magee may wish to contemplate it on his early morning walks up the Windmill Hill."

"I wandered today to the hills, Maggie
To watch the scene below
The creek, and the creaking old mill, Maggie
As we used to long, long ago…"

By the end Maggie had her handkerchief out again and she was joined by some of the other ladies as well. Suddenly, a taxi-driver appeared from no-where and was in the middle of the room announcing:-

"Taxi for Mr. and Mrs. Murphy!"

"That's you, Maggie!" said Turbo, and everyone laughed.

JP and Maggie were getting a taxi to Belfast and the train to Dublin where they were staying for a few days. JP hoped to see Mountjoy Jail where Kevin Barry was executed and Maggie was looking forward to a bit of shopping and the luxury of the Gresham Hotel.

"Jeesus, that filled a hole!" said Turbo as we came out of the Hotel onto the street.

"It'll do ye 'til ye get yer tea anyway," said Finn, "what do ye think yer getting for tea?"

"Probably, mince, carrot and onions."

The married couple were enthusiastically waved-off as the taxi drove away up Castle Street. Father Magee said his goodbyes as he made his way to his car parked just up the street. After the excitement of the day, and with JP and Maggie gone, it was almost anti-climactic. A warm wind blew leaves around our feet as the melancholy of an autumn afternoon descended. Our mothers would go back to their usual chores and we would go back to school. Still, it was a day to be remembered, not least, for JP and Maggie who had waited nearly forty years for it to arrive.

It seemed that Turbo's plan had worked as it was now open season for ball-games round at Maggie's. Until the Saturday afternoon after the wedding, when a game of kerby was in full swing, and the front door flew open.

"Hey, away and play round yer own dures!" it was JP laughing.

"Yer back! How was Dob-blin?" said Finn in his best Dublin accent.

"It was grand. We're just back, and I'm getting a drop o' tay, I'll see ye down the Shore in about half an hour and I'll tell yis all about it."

We hid the ball in the hedge and drifted off towards the Shore. I couldn't help thinking how JP had very subtlety moved us on. We were sitting on the shore wall when we saw JP coming down Ferry Street. He turned left into Blaney's shop and emerged with three 99 ice-creams.

"Splashing out on the ice-creams now," joked Turbo, "it's well seeing that ye've married a rich widow!"

"Y'know how everyone said that Maggie was worth a bob or two, well they were right," said JP, giving out the 99s. "But it was only a bob or two as she didn't actually get the farm. It's traditional in Ireland for land to stay in the family name and it was left to the two brothers. Maggie got a small annual allowance to be paid until such time as she remarried."

"She's lost that now. But we both have the pension and I'll have a bit of a roughness when I sell up out the road. Y'know money isn't everything and sure we're as happy as Peggy the Pig!"

Despite JP's assertion, we were still inclined to get

better acquainted with money, and make up our own minds about it

"Yer moving into town then?" said Finn.

"Aye, sure I'm getting no younger and it's a long oul' trek home on a Saturday night. Maggie's back-garden will do me grand for a few vegetables."

He told us about nearly getting thrown into Mountjoy Jail, which I think was a story he was working on, and about the grubbing in the Gresham which seemed real enough, before moving off to speak to a couple of the old-timers sitting further along the wall.

We sat in silence for a while licking our ice-creams.

"So much for yer grand plan, Turbo," said Finn.

"Ah, I'm fed up with that game anyway. I've a better idea…"

…

ABOUT THE AUTHOR

Author also of Us Boys in Portaferry and Digging Up the Past In Ballyphilip Churchyard.

Printed in Great Britain
by Amazon